P9-CAU-305

1

GREAT ILLUSTRATED CLASSICS

THE ADVENTURES OF
HUCKLEBERRY FINN

Mark Twain

adapted by
Deidre S. Laiken

Illustrations by
Pablo Marcos Studio

ABDO
Publishing Company

GREAT ILLUSTRATED CLASSICS

edited by
Malvina G. Vogel

visit us at
www.abdopub.com

Library edition published in 2002 by ABDO Publishing Company, 4940 Viking Drive, Suite 622, Edina, Minnesota 55435. Published by agreement with Playmore Incorporated Publishers and Waldman Publishing Corporation.

Cover art, interior art, and text copyright © 1990 by Playmore Incorporated Publishers and Waldman Publishing Corporation, New York, New York.

International copyrights reserved in all countries. No part of this book may be reproduced in any form without written permission from the publisher.

Printed in the United States.

Library of Congress Cataloging-in-Publication Data

Twain, Mark, 1835-1910.
  The adventures of Huckelberry Finn / Mark Twain ; adapted by Diedre S. Laiken ; illustrated by Pablo Marcos Studio.
    p. cm – (Great illustrated classics)
  Reprint. Originally published: New York: Playmore: Waldman Pub., 1990.
  Summary: The adventures of a boy and a runaway slave as they float down the Mississippi River on a raft.
    ISBN 1-57765-676-8
  [1. Mississippi River--Fiction. 2. Voyages and travels--Fiction. 3. Friendship--Fiction. 4. Slavery--Fiction. 5. Missouri--History--19th century--Fiction.] I. Laiken, Diedre S. II. Pablos Marcos Studio. III. Title. IV. Series.

PZ7.C584 Ab 2002
[Fic]--dc21

2001056517

Contents

About the Author

Samuel Langhorne Clemens was born in Florida, Missouri, in 1835. Although he left school when he was only twelve years old, he became a man of many interests and occupations. He began his career as a printer, then became a pilot of a Mississippi riverboat. Afterwards, when he worked as a journalist, travel writer, and publisher, Clemens decided to use a pen name. "Mark Twain" came from Clemens' riverboat days, when measuring the depth of the water was called "marking the twain."

Twain has been described as hot-tempered and cynical, but also as tender and sentimental. His love for the past and his feelings for his country helped him produce some of his finest books.

Although Twain wrote many short stories, articles, and novels, including *A Connecticut Yankee in King Arthur's Court*, *The Prince and the Pauper*, and *Life on the Mississippi*, he is probably best remembered for *The Adventures of Tom Sawyer* and *The Adventures of Huckleberry Finn*. Both of these books, Twain admitted, were based on experiences he had in his boyhood and on people he knew as he grew up along the Mississippi River.

Before he died in 1910, Mark Twain—the boy who left school at the age of twelve—received honorary degrees from universities in the United States and in Europe. Today, Mark Twain is remembered and loved as one of America's greatest writers.

Huckleberry Finn

CHAPTER 1

Huck's New Life

You might have heard of me if you read *The Adventures of Tom Sawyer* by Mark Twain. My name is Huckleberry Finn. I have always lived in this same little town of St. Petersburg, Missouri. My father is the town drunk and isn't around much. So I've spent most of my life fishing on the banks of the Mississippi, sleeping in doorways, and having great adventures with my friend Tom Sawyer.

Things were always pretty dull around here until Tom and I discovered hidden treasure. We found twelve thousand dollars *in gold*! It was money that had been buried by robbers, so Judge Thatcher decided it was rightfully ours. Tom and I got six thousand dollars apiece.

The Judge put the money in the bank for us, and we each got an allowance of a dollar a day. For us, in that little town, it was more money than we knew what to do with. But the money didn't make me happy.

At about this time, the Widow Douglas decided to take me in and raise me as her own son. She was kinda grateful, I guess, 'cause I helped save her life. But it was rough living in a house all the time. The Widow made me wash and dress up and eat all my meals at regular hours. She even took me to church. When I couldn't stand it any more, I ran away and got into my old rags. Then I felt free and happy. But Tom Sawyer hunted me up and said he was going to start a club. And

The Widow Takes Huck to Church.

I could only be a member if I went back to living a respectable life with the Widow Douglas.

So I went back, and the Widow cried over me, calling me a "poor lost lamb." She put me in a new suit of clothes that made me feel uncomfortable and sweaty all over again. I had the hardest time getting used to regular meals and polite talk.

Then there was Miss Watson, the Widow's sister, who had just come to live with her. She took an immediate interest in me and tried to teach me to read and spell. These lessons jut made me tired and lonesome. By and by, she would send me to bed with a piece of candle for light.

One night after my lesson, I felt so unhappy there, I wished I was dead. I sat in the quiet house and listened for the sound of the wind or the rustle of the trees. After a while, I heard a "Meow! Meow!" coming from

Lessons Make Huck Tired.

beneath my window.

It was Tom's signal. He had called a midnight meeting of our club. I answered his signal with my own "Meow." Then I slipped into my clothes very quietly and was out the window in a flash.

We all met by a clump of bushes not far from the Widow's house. There was me and Tom and Ben Rogers and Tommy Barnes and Joe Harper. We talked for a little while, and then we all took an oath of loyalty to the club. We elected Tom captain and Joe Harper second captain, and then we started home.

I climbed up the shed and crept into my window just before daybreak. My new clothes were greased-up and full of clay, and I was dog-tired.

An Oath of Loyalty

The Widow Cleans Huck's Clothes.

CHAPTER 2

Pap Returns

Well, I got a good going-over in the morning from old Miss Watson because of my clothes, but the Widow didn't scold me. She just cleaned off the grease and clay and looked so sorry that I thought I would behave if I could, at least for a little while.

After three or four months had passed, our little club broke up, and we all started school again. It was the first time for me, but I could already spell and read and write and do a little arithmetic.

At first I hated school, but the more I went,

the easier it got. I sort of got used to the Widow's ways, but living in a house and sleeping in a bed made me feel a little *too* civilized. So, before the cold weather came on, I slept outside whenever I could slip away. It made the house easier to take.

One morning I happened to drop the salt shaker at breakfast. This was sure to be my bad luck day. I went down to the front yard and climbed over the high board fence. There was an inch of new snow on the ground, and I stopped when I saw some fresh tracks. Whoever made them had come up from the quarry and stood around the fence for a while, then went on around the garden. It was funny he hadn't come in, after standing around. I couldn't figure it out. It was very strange somehow. I was about to follow the tracks when something stopped me. The impression made in the snow by the left boot heel was in the shape of a cross. It was

16

Fresh Tracks in the Snow!

formed by two big nails imbedded crossways into the heel—a good luck sign.

I had seen that heel print before. . . ! Suddenly, I was up and running down the hill as fast as my legs could carry me. I looked over my shoulder every few seconds, but I didn't see anyone. I reached Judge Thatcher's house in a few minutes.

"Why Huck, you're all out of breath," he said as he opened the door. "Did you come for your interest?"

"No, sir," I answered "Is there some?"

"Oh yes, a half-yearly check came in last night—over a hundred fifty dollars. Quite a fortune for you. You had better let me invest it for you along with your six thousand."

"No, sir," I explained breathlessly. "I don't want you to invest it. I want you to take it—the interest and the six thousand too!"

The Judge looked surprised. He couldn't figure me out. "Why do you want me to take

A Familiar Heel Print!

The Adventures of Huckleberry Finn

it, Huck? What can you mean by giving away all your money like this?"

"Please don't ask me any more questions, sir. I know what I'm doing all right."

After a while, I convinced the Judge that I meant what I said. He asked me to sign a paper to make it all legal. I did it and left.

I hurried back to the Widow's. At least there, I'd be safe. Once inside, I lit my candle and went up to my room. I shut the door and breathed a big sigh of relief. But then I turned around...there he was! Pap. I used to be scared of him all the time because he hit me so much when he was drunk and all. But now I took a good look at the old man, and he didn't look that frightening at all.

He was almost fifty, and he looked it. His hair was long and black, no gray. But it was tangled and greasy and hung down into his long, mixed-up whiskers. You could see his eyes shining through like he was behind

Huck Signs a Legal Paper.

vines. There wasn't any color in his face. It was white, but not like another man's white. It was a white that could make a person sick, a white to make a person's flesh crawl. He was sitting on my bed with one ankle resting on the other knee. The boot on his raised foot was busted, and two of his toes stuck through. His clothes were all in rags, and his old black slouch hat with the top caved in was laying on the floor near his feet.

We stared at each other, then Pap looked me up and down. "Fancy clothes you got there," he said. "You think you're a big shot now, don't you?"

"Maybe I am and maybe I'm not," I answered.

"Don't you give me any of your lip," he snorted. "You've put on airs since I've been away. I'll take you down a peg or two before I'm done with you. I hear you can read and write now too. I bet you think you're better

Pap!

than your own father now, don't you? Who told you you could meddle with such foolishness, huh? Who told you?"

I explained to Pap that the Widow wanted me to learn how to read and write and dress and live like a civilized human being.

"It's that widow out to steal my own son," he cried. "But no mind, where's the money?"

I told him that I gave it all to Judge Thatcher, but he didn't believe me.

"I'll go see the judge," he said angrily, "and find out where the money is and get my hands on it one way or the other." Then he made me empty my pockets, and he took the dollar the judge had given me. I knew he'd go downtown to buy some whiskey.

The next day he was drunk, and he went to see Judge Thatcher. He shouted and threatened that he'd get the law on the judge if he didn't give him the money. When the judge refused, Pap went to court.

Pap Makes Huck Empty His Pockets.

Pap Grabs Huck.

CHAPTER 3

Escape

The trial went slowly, so every now and then I had to borrow some money from the judge to give to Pap. Whenever he got the money, he got drunk and made a big commotion in town. Then he was thrown in jail. This happened again and again.

He got to hanging around the Widow's so much that she told him if he didn't quit it, she would make trouble for him. This got the old man real angry. So he watched for me, and one day in the spring he grabbed me.

He took me up the river about three miles

and crossed over to the Illinois shore where it was woody and deserted with no houses. We walked through the woods until we came to the old log cabin where we once lived.

For the next few months, we lived on the food we hunted and fished. Every once in a while Pap locked me in the cabin and went to the store to trade fish and game for whiskey. He'd fetch it home and get drunk. Then he'd lock the door at night and put the key under his head alongside his gun.

But by and by, Pap got too handy with his belt when he got drunk, and I couldn't stand it. I was covered with welts. He got to going away a lot too, and he would lock me in the cabin so I couldn't escape.

Once, he locked me in and was gone for three days. I was terribly lonesome and scared. I thought maybe he had drowned, and I was sure I would never get out again. I had to figure out some way to escape. I had

Heading For the Old Log Cabin

tried to get out of that cabin many a time, but I just couldn't figure out how. When Pap was away, he was pretty careful not to leave a knife or anything in the cabin for me to cut through the floor. The windows weren't big enough for even a dog to get through, the chimney was too narrow to climb up, and the door was made of thick solid oak slabs.

Finally I found an old rusty saw with a broken handle. I fixed the handle and looked for a place to start sawing. There, behind a table at the far end of the cabin, was an old horse blanket nailed against the log wall. I got under the table, raised the blanket, and went to work sawing out a section of the big bottom log for me to escape through.

Well, it was a long job, but I was getting towards the end when I heard Pap's gun in the woods. I got rid of the signs of my work, dropped the blanket over the hole, and hid my saw. Pretty soon Pap came in.

Sawing His Way Out

He was in his usual mood—a bad one. He said he had been downtown, and everything was going wrong. His lawyer said the trial would take a long time, and there would be no money until the court made a decision.

Meanwhile, the Widow had been looking for me. She had sent a man to try to follow Pap, but Pap drove him off with his shotgun. After that, he threatened to hide me in another place where no one would find me. So I decided that if I could keep Pap *and* the Widow from trying to find me, then I would *really* be free.

After we had dinner, Pap locked me up in the cabin and went back to town. I judged he wouldn't come back that night, so I waited until he had a good start, then I pulled out my saw. Before he was on the other side of the river, the hole was finished, and I was out.

I knew where there was an old canoe tied

Pap Drives a Man Off.

up on the shore, so I took a sack of cornmeal, a side of bacon, some sugar, and coffee, and headed down to the river. I filled the canoe with string, matches, a tin cup, and some blankets. Then I went back to the cabin and covered up the hole I had made.

As part of my plan, I took Pap's shotgun from its hiding place, then went into the woods and shot a pig. I found Pap's axe and used it to smash the cabin door to bits. Next, I fetched the pig inside, cut open its throat, and let it's blood make a trail wherever I dragged it.

Then I pulled out some of my hair and stuck it and the axe on the cabin door. The whole thing looked like someone had hacked his way into the cabin, killed me, and dragged my body off somewhere.

When it was dark, I moved the canoe down the river and waited under some willows for the moon to rise. I took a bite to eat and by

34

Huck Sets a Murder Scene.

and by laid down in the canoe to smoke my pipe and figure out a plan. I knew the townspeople would drag the river for my body, but they would soon get tired of that. Maybe they would hunt for the robbers who broke into the cabin. But right now, I needed to find some place to hide. So I decided to head for Jackson's Island. I knew the place pretty well.

When the moon rose, I pushed off in the canoe, and soon I was on my way. It didn't take long to get to the island. Once I landed and tied up my canoe, I headed for the big log at the head of the island. From there, I could see way over to town, three miles away. The lights were twinkling, and if I closed my eyes, I could almost see the Widow Douglas inside the big house on the hill.

There was a little gray in the sky now as dawn came on, so I stepped into the woods and laid down for a nap before breakfast.

Pushing Off from Shore

Rested and Satisfied

CHAPTER 4

Finding Jim

The sun was so high in the sky when I woke up that I figured it was after eight o'clock. I lay there on the grass in the cool shade, looking up at the sun through the holes in the branches. I felt rested and satisfied. A couple of squirrels sat on a limb and jabbered at me in a friendly way.

I was lazy and comfortable and didn't even want to get up to cook breakfast. So I started dozing of again, when suddenly I heard a deep booming sound. It came from way up the river. I sat up and rested on my elbow, listening. Pretty soon I heard it again. I jumped up and ran down to the river. A ferryboat full of people was heading towards the island.

Suddenly, I knew what was happening. They were firing a cannon over the water because they believed it would make a drowned body come to the top, and they were searching for mine.

I stood hidden in the bushes, watching the cannon smoke and listening to the booms. I lit a pipe and had a good long smoke while I went on watching. By and by, the boat drifted so close to the shore that I could have almost touched it. I saw most everybody on the boat—Pap and Judge Thatcher, Joe Harper and Tom Sawyer, and plenty more. I could hear them all talking about a murder—*my murder*!

Suddenly, the captain called out, "Look sharp now! The current sets in the closest

Huck Spies the Ferryboat.

here, and maybe he's washed ashore and got tangled amongst the brush at the water's edge. I hope so anyway."

I didn't hope so. Everybody crowded up and leaned over the rails, nearly in my face. They kept still, watching with all their might.

When they didn't find anything, they gave up and headed back towards town.

I knew I was all right now. Nobody else would come hunting for me. I got my traps out of the canoe and made a nice camp in the thick woods. I set up a tent out of my blankets so I'd have a place to put my things where the rain couldn't get at them. Then I caught a catfish and roasted it over a fire.

When it was dark, I sat by my campfire, smoking and feeling pretty well satisfied. After a while, it got sort of lonesome, so I listened to the current swashing along and counted the stars until I fell asleep.

And so it was for three days and nights. No

Looking for a Body

difference—just the same thing. But on the fourth day, I went exploring around the island—*my* island. I was boss of it. It all belonged to me, so to say, and I wanted to know all about it. I was walking along when all of a sudden in a clearing, I bounded right onto the ashes of a campfire. They were still warm!

My heart jumped up into my lungs. I never waited to look further, but uncocked my gun and went sneaking back to my camp as quiet and as fast as I could. Every now and then I stopped for a second amongst the thick leaves and listened again.

As soon as I got back to my camp, I put out the fire, hid my traps, and climbed up in a tree. I reckon I was up in the tree two hours, but I didn't see or hear a thing.

Well, I couldn't stay up there forever, so at last I climbed down. By that time it was dark, and I was pretty hungry. But I didn't dare make a fire, so I went to sleep hungry.

A Campfire on Huck's Island!

I didn't sleep much. I couldn't somehow, because I was thinking all the time. By and by, I said to myself, "I can't live this way. I'm going to find out who's here on the island with me. I'll find it out or bust."

So I began searching all around the island, and after a while, I caught a glimpse of a fire through the trees. I went towards it, slowly and cautiously. Soon I was close enough to have a look, and there, on the ground lay a man. He had a blanket over most of his body, and his head was nearly in the fire. Pretty soon he yawned and stretched. Then he threw off the blanket.

It was Jim—Miss Watson's slave! At that time in Missouri it was still legal to have slaves, and Jim and I had gotten to be friends when I had lived at the Widow's. I sure was glad to see him.

"Hello, Jim!" I said, skipping out of the bushes.

Jim—Miss Watson's Slave

He jumped up and stared at me with a wild look. Then he dropped down on his knees and gasped, "Don't hurt me, don't! I never hurt a ghost. I always liked dead people. You go get back in the river where you belong."

Well, it took some talking, but I finally made him understand that I wasn't dead. I was ever so glad to see Jim. I wasn't lonesome now. I talked on and on, telling Jim everything that had happened to me. But Jim only sat there looking at me and never saying one word.

Finally we went over to where the canoe was tied up, and while Jim built a fire in a grassy open place among the trees, I fetched some meal, bacon, coffee, and sugar from the boat. We cooked breakfast, and when it was ready, we lolled on the grass and ate it.

Jim laid into it with all his might, for he was almost starved. Then when he had gotten pretty well stuffed, he relaxed and

"Don't Hurt Me!"

said, "Listen here, Huck, I got to tell you why I'm here, but you must never tell a soul."

After I promised, Jim told me his story. "Well, Huck, I had to run off," he said. "Miss Watson, she picked on me all the time and treated me poorly, but she always said she wouldn't sell me down to New Orleans. But I noticed there was a slave trader around the place a lot, and I began to get uneasy. Well, one night I crept home late, and I heard Miss Watson tell the Widow that she was going to sell me down to New Orleans for eight hundred dollars. It was so much money, she just couldn't resist. The Widow tried to talk her out of it, but I got so scared, I never waited to hear the rest. I lit out mighty quick, I tell you."

So for the past week, Jim was in hiding too. We both agreed that it was good to have company, and we set about fishing for our lunch.

Jim Tells Why He Ran Away.

A Catfish As Big As a Man!

CHAPTER 5

The Woman Helps Huck

Well, the days went along, and the river rose over its banks, then went down again. It was a good time for fishing. We baited one of the big hooks with a skinned rabbit and caught us a catfish as big as a man. It was six feet two inches long and weighed over two hundred pounds. It was as big a fish as was ever caught in the Mississippi, I reckon. Jim said he hadn't ever seen a bigger one.

We couldn't haul him in, of course. He would have pulled the two of us into the river. We just sat there, watching him tear around and around until he got tired and drowned.

When we cut him open, we found a brass button, a round ball, and lots of rubbish in his stomach. We split the ball open with a hatchet and found a spool inside. Jim said the spool had to have been inside the ball a long time for it to be coated over and made into a ball.

A fish like this would have been worth a lot of money in the village. Its snow-white meat is sold by the pound and makes a good fish fry. And it was all ours!

Next morning, life was getting slow and dull, and I wanted to get excited about something or other. I decided to slip over across the river and find out what was going on. Jim liked the idea, but he said I should go in the dark and be very careful.

Then he thought a while and came up with a better idea. A few days earlier when the

Cutting Open the Catfish

water was rising, parts of a wrecked house came floating by us on the river. Jim had managed to salvage some of the contents of the house. Among them were a girl's dress and sunbonnet. Jim thought that if I dressed like a girl, it would be the perfect disguise. I thought so too. So I rolled my trouser legs up to my knees and got into the dress. Jim hitched it from behind with the little hooks. It was a pretty good fit. Then I put on the sunbonnet and tied it under my chin. Jim said nobody would know me, even in the daytime. I practiced moving around in the clothes all day to get the hang of things, and by and by I could do pretty well in them. But Jim said I didn't walk like girls usually do, and he told me to stop pulling up my dress to get at my pant's pocket. I kept that in mind and did better.

I started up the Illinois shore in the canoe just before dark and landed at a town a little

Huck's Perfect Disguise

below the ferry landing. After I tied up the canoe, I began walking along the bank towards a little shanty. There was a light burning in a window, so I slipped up and peeped in.

A woman about forty years old was inside, knitting by the light of a candle on a pine table beside her. She had to be a stranger in town, for I didn't know her. There wasn't a face in that little town that I didn't know. This was a lucky break for me. Since she was new in town, she wouldn't know me either, and I could find out all the things I was itching to know.

I knocked at the door and reminded myself that I was supposed to be a girl.

"Come in," said the woman, smiling. "And what might your name be?"

"Sarah Williams," I answered in a high voice.

"Where do you live? In this neighborhood?"

Huck Peeps into the Shanty.

"No, ma'am. In Hookerville, seven miles down the river. I've walked all the way, and I'm all tired out."

"Hungry, too, I reckon."

"No, ma'am. I was so hungry before that I had to stop two miles below here at a farm. But I'm not hungry any more. My mother's down sick and out of money and everything, and I've come to tell my uncle, Abner Moore. He lives at the other end of town. So if it's all right with you, I'd just like to sit here and rest a while."

She said she wouldn't let me go all that way by myself, but if I'd wait a while, her husband would be home soon, and he'd walk me there. Then she got to talking about her husband and her family and about how much better off they used to be—and so on and so on. At this point, I was beginning to think that I had made a mistake coming to her to find out what was going on in the town. All I

The Woman Invites Huck In.

found out was about her and her family.

But after a while she began to talk about Pap and the murder, and then I was pretty willing to let her chatter right along. She told me about Tom Sawyer finding the twelve thousand dollars and about Pap and what a disgrace he was and about what a problem Huck was. At last, she got down to where I was murdered.

"Who did it?" I asked.

"Probably old Finn, himself," she said. "Almost everyone thought that at first. He'll never know how close he came to being hanged. But before nightfall, people changed their minds and decided it was done by a runaway slave named Jim."

"Why he...." But I stopped right there. I reckoned I had better keep still. She kept on talking and never noticed that I had said anything at all.

"The slave ran off the very night Huck

Talking About Pap and the Murder

Finn was killed," she went on. "So there's a reward out for him—three hundred dollars. And there's a reward out for old Finn too—two hundred dollars.

"You see, old Finn came to town the morning after the murder and told what he had found at his cabin. He went with the townspeople on the ferryboat hunt, and right away after that, he just upped and left town. Before night they wanted to hang him, but he was gone, you see.

"Well, the next day, they found out the slave was gone too. So they put the blame on him. Then the day after, old Finn came back and went boo-hooing to Judge Thatcher to get money to hunt for the slave. The judge gave him some, and that evening old Finn got drunk. He was around town until after midnight with a couple of rough-looking strangers, and then he went off with them.

"Well, he hasn't been back since, and they

Old Finn Got Drunk.

aren't looking for him until this thing blows over a little. People now think that he killed his own son and fixed things so that folks would think robbers did it. Then he'd get Huck's money without having to bother with a lawsuit and all. Everyone says that was a horrible thing to do. Oh, he's sly all right. You can't prove anything against him, you know. If he doesn't come back for a year, he'll be safe. Everything will be quieted down by then, and he'll walk into Huck's money as easy as can be."

"And does everyone still think the slave killed Huck?" I asked.

"Not everyone, but a good many do, and I'm one of them. In fact, I think I even know where the slave is hiding."

Then the woman began to tell how she had seen some smoke coming from Jackson's Island. She knew that no one lived there, so she figured that's where the runaway slave

Seeing Smoke from Jackson's Island

had been hiding. Since there was a three hundred-dollar reward out for Jim, she had just sent her husband to search the island.

I got so uneasy when I heard this that I couldn't sit still. I had to do something with my hands, so I took up a needle and began threading it. When the woman stopped talking, I looked up. She was looking at me in a curious way and smiling a little. Pretty soon she asked, "What did you say your name was, honey?"

"M-Mary Williams," I stammered.

"Honey, I thought you said it was Sarah when you first came in."

"Oh, yes I did. Sarah Mary Williams. Sarah's my first name. Some people call me Mary."

I was feeling better then, but I wished I was out of there anyway. Pretty soon she went and got a long hank of yarn which she wanted me to help her with. I held up my

Trying to Thread a Needle

two hands. She put the hank over them and began to wind the yarn into a ball. She went on talking about her family and all. But I was more interested in watching a couple of rats stick their noses out of a hole in the corner.

Suddenly the woman stopped what she was doing and said, "Keep your eye on your work, young lady."

At that moment she dropped the ball of yarn into my lap, and I clapped my legs together on it. The woman looked at the way I had caught the yarn, then she looked me straight in the face. "Come now, what's your real name?" she demanded. "Bill? Tom? Bob? I know you're a boy."

I pretended to play dumb, but it was no use. She could tell by the way I wound the yarn and the way I clapped my legs together that I wasn't a girl.

I knew it was no use pretending I was a

Huck Catches the Yarn.

girl, so I put my mind to work figuring out another story. I explained that I was an orphan, and the law had bound me out to a mean old farmer in the country. He treated me so badly that I just had to run away. I stole some of his daughter's clothes and just pretended to be a girl so that I wouldn't get caught.

"But I really do have an uncle in this town," I added, "and I'm going to try to find him."

Anyway, she believed me and packed me up a fine snack to eat on my way back to town. I said good-bye to her and as quickly as I could, I slipped back to where the canoe was hidden. I jumped in and was off in a hurry.

As soon as I reached the island, I didn't wait a minute. Just remembering my conversation with the woman made me nervous. She had told me that her husband was on his way to see if Jim was hiding out on the

A Fine Snack for Huck

island. I jumped out of the canoe and ran towards our camp.

"Get up, Jim," I shouted. "There's not a minute to lose! They're after us!"

Jim never asked a single question. The way he worked for the next half-hour showed just how frightened he really was. Soon, everything we had in the world was on our raft, and it was ready to be shoved out from the willow cove where he had hidden it.

I took the canoe out from shore and tied it onto the raft. Soon we were slipping along in the shade, past the foot of the island, never saying a word.

"There's Not a Minute to Lose!"

Covering the Raft with Branches

CHAPTER 6

Murderer on the Wrecked Steamboat

It must have been close to one o'clock when we got below the island. The raft seemed to go mighty slow. All I could think of was how close we'd come to getting discovered.

When the first streak of day began to show, we tied up to a rock on the Illinois side and covered the raft with cottonwood branches. We didn't want to take any chances that someone might discover us. We hid on shore until dark, then we pulled out the raft and drifted down the wide river. We did this every day for four days, hiding by day and drifting at night. We passed towns along the bank and towns up on the black hillsides. They looked like shiny beds of lights twinkling in the darkness.

The fifth night adrift, we passed St. Louis. It was like the whole world lit up. I had heard about St. Louis, but I had never believed any place could be so big or so bright.

Every night I would slip ashore at about ten o'clock and buy ten or fifteen cents worth of meal or bacon or something to eat. Sometimes I helped myself to a chicken that wasn't roosting very comfortably.

Mornings before daylight, I slipped into cornfields and borrowed a watermelon or a muskmelon or a pumpkin or some new corn. Pap had always said it wasn't any harm to borrow things if you meant to return them someday.

Around midnight on the fifth night below St. Louis, we had a big storm. There was a

Borrowing Watermelon and Corn

lot of thunder and lightning, and we stayed inside a tent on top of the raft. By and by, I saw a steamboat that had crashed into a rock. We were drifting straight towards it. When the lightning flashed, I could see the boat clearly. It was leaning over, with part of the upper deck above water.

Well, it being the middle of the night and stormy, I felt like any other boy would have—excited! I wanted to get aboard the steamboat and slink around a little.

Jim was dead set against it. "I don't want to go fooling around with no wreck," he said, and he grumbled for a little while. But I managed to convince him that it was the thing to do.

The deck was easy to get onto, so we jumped right on board. We went sneaking along, when suddenly we heard a voice cry out, "Oh, please don't, boys! I swear I won't ever tell!"

A Wrecked Steamboat!

Another voice said, "It's a lie, Bill Turner. You've acted this way before. You always want more than your share of the loot. And you've always got it too. But this time you've said just one word too many. You're the meanest, most treacherous hound in this country."

I turned around to Jim, but he was gone. He had run straight for the raft. I was too curious to leave now, so I dropped to my hands and knees in the little passage and crept along in the dark, heading closer and closer to the voices.

I came to an open door and peeked into the room. There, on the floor I saw a man stretched out, tied hand and foot. Two men were standing over him, pointing a pistol at his head. The prisoner was begging for mercy, repeating over and over that he would never tell and pleading with the man he called "Packard." Finally, Packard explained

A Prisoner Begs for Mercy.

to his partner that he didn't want to kill the man. He had a better plan which he would discuss when they were alone.

The two men went off into another room. I flattened myself against the wall as they passed by me in the darkness, then I followed them to the other room. I put my ear to the wall and listened.

"My idea is this," said Packard. "We'll rustle around and gather up whatever things we've overlooked in the stateroom. Then we'll shove for shore and hide the loot... and wait. It won't be more than two hours before this wreck breaks up and washes off down the river. See? He'll be drowned and won't have anyone to blame for it but himself. I think that's better than killing him ourselves."

Packard's partner agreed, and they started gathering their loot. I took off in a cold sweat and headed for the raft. But I stumbled over

Huck Listens to the Men's Plans.

Jim, lying stretched out on the edge of the deck.

"Quick Jim! There isn't any time for fooling around and pretending to sleep. There's a gang of murderers on this wreck, and if we don't find their boat and set it drifting down the river, they'll get away! Quick, hurry! Let's start looking! You start at the raft, and...."

"Oh, my lord!" whispered Jim, looking over the rail. "There isn't any raft. It broke loose and it's gone!"

I caught my breath and almost fainted. We were trapped on a wreck with two murderers. With our raft gone, we just had to find their boat and take it for ourselves. So we started our search.

After a few minutes, Jim spotted the boat tied up to the stern of the wreck. It was piled high with loot the robbers had taken from the steamboat. I was pretty thankful that he was able to find it in the pitch dark. In half a

The Raft Is Gone!

second I was in the boat, and Jim came tumbling after me. I cut the rope that held us to the wreck, and away we went!

When we were three or four hundred yards downstream, we saw Packard's lantern appear on deck, shining like a little spark. They must have discovered that their boat was gone and realized that they were in as much trouble as their prisoner.

Jim manned the oars, and we began to hunt for our raft. For the first time, I began to worry about the men and how dreadful it was, even for murders to be in such a fix. So I said to Jim, "The first light we see, we'll land and find a good hiding place for you and the raft. Then I'll think of some kind of a story so I can get someone to go and rescue the gang. That way, they can be hanged when their time comes."

But that idea was a failure because it soon began to storm again. The rain poured down

Leaving the Wreck

so heavily that we couldn't see any lights at all. The wind pushed us along down the river, while we watched for lights and looked for our raft.

After a long while the rain let up, but the clouds stayed. The lightning showed us a black thing ahead. It was the raft. We made straight for it.

When we pulled alongside the raft, we began unloading some of the loot from the the boat and piling it in a great heap on our little raft. There were boots, blankets, and all sorts of clothing. Jim even found a box of cigars. We hadn't been this rich in our lives.

After we had unloaded all the loot, I told Jim to float along down the river and shine a light when he figured he had gone about two miles. Then he was to keep the light burning until I came. Meanwhile, I would be manning the oars of the boat and heading towards shore.

Loading the Loot onto the Raft

The Adventures of Huckleberry Finn

When I reached the bank, I tied up the boat and headed for the small village I saw twinkling in the darkness. The first person I met was a watchman. As soon as I saw him, I began crying. I made up a story about how the steamboat had crashed and how my family was stranded there. Since I was the only one who could swim, I told him, they had sent me to save them. I promised the watchman that my family would reward him well for saving their lives.

After I had finished my story, the old man got his boat ready for the rescue mission. I crept away in the darkness and waited in the boat on shore for Jim's signal. But I couldn't rest easy until I saw the watchman's boat heading for the wreck. I was feeling kind of proud of myself for taking so much trouble for that gang.

Well, before long, I could see the wreck, dim and dusky, sliding along down into the

Huck Asks a Watchman for Help.

river. A cold shiver went through me. There wasn't much chance now that anybody could survive.

It seemed a long time before Jim's light showed up. When I finally saw it, I rowed towards it. By the time I got there, the sky was beginning to get a little gray in the east. We tied the boat to the raft and struck out for an island in the river. When we reached it, we hid the raft behind some bushes and sank the boat. When this was done, we turned in and slept like two dead people.

The Wreck Slides into the River.

Spending a Few Days in the Woods

CHAPTER 7

The King and the Duke

After our adventure with the gang, Jim and I decided to take it easy for a while and spend a few days in the woods. I told him what had happened inside the wreck and on shore. He said that when he discovered the raft was gone, he nearly died. He figured it was all over for him anyway. If no one saved him, he would be sure to drown. And if someone had found him, they would take him back to the village to get the reward. Then Miss Watson would sell him down south for sure. I knew he was right about all that, and we both realized how lucky we had been.

After a few days in the woods, we got back on the raft and headed down the river once again. Sometimes we'd have that whole river to ourselves for the longest time. It's lovely to live on a raft. We had the sky up there, all speckled with stars, and we would lay on our backs, looking up at them and discussing whether they were made or only just happened. Jim was sure the stars were made, but I said I thought they just happened.

Once or twice during the night, we would see a steamboat slipping along in the dark. Now and then it would belch a whole world of sparks out of its chimneys, and the sparks would rain down on the river. Then the boat would turn a bend, and its lights would wink out. A long time after the steamboat was gone, the waves would get to us and joggle the raft a bit. Then, there would be nothing but silence.

Discussing Stars

The Adventures of Huckleberry Finn

One morning about daybreak, I found a canoe drifting near the main shore. I got into it and paddled over to the shore to look for berries. After I landed, I was following a cow path across a creek when I saw a couple of men running towards me. I was about to run in the other direction, but they called out to me.

"Save us! Please save us!" they cried. "We haven't done anything wrong, but we're being chased by men and dogs."

I felt sorry for them, so I led them back to the canoe. We climbed aboard, and as I rowed, I studied the two men.

One of them was about seventy years old. He had a bald head and very gray whiskers. The other fellow was about thirty and pretty ordinary-looking. Both men's clothes were all wrinkled, but fancy-looking, and they carried big fat carpetbags.

I rowed them out to the raft where we all

"Please Save Us!"

had breakfast, then we relaxed and talked. The first thing that came out was that these two fellows didn't know each other, but both had gotten into trouble. The bald-headed man had been selling medicine that was supposed to take the tartar off people's teeth. The trouble was that it took off the enamel along with it.

The younger man had been running temperance meetings where he lectured folks about the evil of drinking. The people loved him, and he had been making up to ten dollars a night. Then he got caught drinking, himself, and he had to run for his life.

Well, the two men got to talking, and they decided that they should team up in business and travel up and down the river together. They began making all sorts of plans.

Suddenly, in the middle of their conversation, the younger man began to weep.

"My poor heart is broken," he cried, "for I

The Two Men Team Up in Business.

have fallen so low from such a high position in life." Then he cleared his throat, wiped the corner of his eye with a rag, and said solemnly, "Gentlemen, I reveal a great secret to you all. By rights, I am a duke! My great-grandfather, the eldest son of the Duke of Bridgewater, came to this country at the end of the last century. His younger brother stayed in England and seized the duke's title and estate upon the nobleman's death even though they should have been passed onto my grandfather, my father, and me. So you see, I am the rightful Duke of Bridgewater. Yet here I am, forlorn, torn from my high estate, despised by the cold world, ragged, worn, heartbroken, and living on a raft!"

Jim pitied him ever so much. So did I. We tried to comfort him, but it wasn't much use. All he asked was that we bow to him, wait on him, and call him "Your Grace" or "My Lord." Then he added that plain "Bridgewater"

"I Am the Rightful Duke of Bridgewater."

would be okay too.

Well, that was easy, so we did it. All through dinner we stood around and waited on him. After a while, the other man—the old, baldheaded one—got pretty quiet. He didn't seem to like all the special treatment the duke was getting.

"Looky here, Bilgewater," he said, "I'm sorry for you, but you aren't the only person with these troubles. You see, I, too, have a secret, Bilgewater. I am a king! I am *Looey the Seventeen*, son of *Looey the Sixteen* and *Marry Antonette of France*!"

"You? At your age" cried the duke. "That's impossible! You must be the late Charlemagne, for you look at least six or seven hundred years old!"

"Trouble has done it, Bilgewater. Trouble has brought these gray hairs and this premature baldness," sobbed the old man.

Well, he cried and carried on so, that Jim

"I Am a King!"

hardly knew what to do. We felt for him, but we felt proud too. It isn't everyday that ordinary people get to meet royalty. Then the king asked that we treat him special too. He wanted to be called "Your Majesty" and to be waited on at meals. So Jim and I started treating him special too.

All this got the duke pretty upset. He wanted to be the only special one but now he had to share everything with the king. Still, the king acted real friendly towards him and said that all the Dukes of Bilgewater were thought a good deal of by his father, *Looey the Sixteen.*

The duke stayed huffy a good while, till by and by the king said "Like it or not, we've got to be together on this raft for a long time. What's the use of you being so sour? We've got a good thing going here, plenty of food and an easy life. Let's shake hands and be friends."

The Duke Is Pretty Upset.

The Adventures of Huckleberry Finn

The duke shook his hand, and Jim and I were pretty glad to see it. It would have been uncomfortable to have any bad feelings on a raft. The most important thing is for everyone to be friendly and feel right and kind towards each other.

It didn't take me long to make up my mind that these men weren't kings or dukes at all. They were just low-down, lying frauds. But I decided it would be best not to say a word about it. That way, there would be no quarrels, and no one would get into any trouble. If they wanted us to call them kings and dukes, I had no objections. As long as it kept peace in the family, I didn't mind. There was no sense in telling Jim either. He was so excited about knowing royalty and all, it would only make him feel badly if he knew these two were fakes. About the only thing I ever learned from Pap was to let certain kinds of people have their own way.

The Duke and King Shake Hands.

Waiting on the King and Duke

CHAPTER 8

The Royal Nonesuch

Well, a couple of days passed, and Jim and I continued to wait on the king and the duke. Afer a while, the king got bored with just drifting down the river, and he and the duke began to plan their next caper.

"The first town we come to," said the duke, "we'll hire a hall and put on a play—maybe something from Shakespeare."

The king explained that he didn't know anything about acting, but the duke told him not to worry. So for the next couple of hours they practiced. It didn't seem much like a play to me, but I knew the duke had some sort of trick in mind.

There was a little town about three miles down the bend, and after lunch, the duke said he wanted to stop there. Since we were out of coffee, I decided to go along into town too. Jim stayed on the raft and waited for us.

When we got to the town, there wasn't anyone stirring. The streets were empty and dead. We found one old man sunning himself in his backyard, and we asked him where everyone was. He said the whole town had gone to a camp meeting about two miles into the woods. The king decided to go have a look while the duke and I headed for the printing office.

After searching several streets, we finally found it, hidden away in a dusty side street. It was a dirty, cluttered-up place covered with ink marks and littered with handbills. The door was unlocked, so the duke just

Empty, Deserted Streets

invited himself inside. He told me to go ahead to the camp meeting. He had things to do.

The camp meeting was crowded, and the sun was awful hot. The king had gotten himself a little platform in one of the tents, and he was preaching his heart out. He was also passing the plate. Last time I looked, he had almost seven dollars.

A few hours later I returned to the printing shop. The duke was standing outside holding a bunch of handbills he had just printed up. The handbills said:

AT THE COURTHOUSE—FOR THREE NIGHTS ONLY!
THE WORLD FAMOUS TRAGEDIANS
DAVID GARRICK, THE YOUNGER &
EDMUND KEAN, THE ELDER
IN THEIR THRILLING TRAGEDY
THE KING'S CAMELEOPARD OR
THE ROYAL NONESUCH!

admission 50¢

The King Preaches His Heart Out.

The duke had me post some of the hand-bills all over town. Then he sent me back to the camp meeting to hand out the rest.

Towards evening, I went back to the raft and found the duke and the king already there. Jim was serving them dinner, and they were plotting and planning for the next day.

Early the next morning, we returned to town. The duke and the king worked real hard rigging up a stage, a curtain, and a row of candles for footlights. The courthouse looked mighty fancy when they were through.

That night the house was jam full of people. When the place couldn't hold another person, the duke quit tending the door and went around the back way. He got on the stage, stood up in front of the curtain, and made a little speech. He praised the tragedy and said it was the most thrilling one that ever was. He just went on bragging about the tragedy

Candles for Footlights

and about the star, Edmund Kean, the Elder. Finally, when everyone's expectations were high enough, he rolled up the curtain. The next minute the king came prancing out on stage on all fours. His naked body was painted with stripes of all sorts of colors. The outfit was wild and kind of funny. The people almost killed themselves laughing. When the king was finished crawling around and making faces, the people roared and clapped and stormed and haw-hawed until he came back and did it all over again. After that, they made him do it another time.

Then the duke let down the curtain, bowed to the people, and said that the great tragedy would be performed only two more nights. He asked everybody to tell their friends about it, so that they, too, would have this wonderful experience.

Twenty people shouted out, "What? Is it over? Is that all?"

The King Prances on the Stage.

When the duke answered yes, everybody stood up and shouted, "Cheat!" They began heading for the stage, but a big, fine-looking man jumped up on a bench and shouted, "Hold on, folks! Just a word! We were cheated mightly badly, but we don't want to be the laughing stock of the whole town. I reckon we'll never hear the last of this thing as long as we live. No, what we want is to go out of here quietly and talk this show up and let the rest of the town be taken! Then we'll all be in the same boat. Isn't that sensible? We should all go home and advise everybody to come and see the tragedy."

The crowd thought this was a good idea, and they all left quietly.

Next day, you couldn't hear anything around town except how wonderful that show was. The house was jammed again that night, and the duke sold this crowd the same way he had sold the last.

"Cheat!"

The Adventures of Huckleberry Finn

When we got back to the raft after the show, we all had supper. Then the duke and the king made Jim and me back the raft out and float it down the middle of the river. We had to hide it about two miles below town. We didn't understand why, but we couldn't question them.

The third night, the house was packed again, but it was packed with all the people who had been at the show the night before. I stood at the door with the duke, and I could see that every man who entered had his pockets bulging. I could smell rotten eggs, cabbages, and all sorts of foul things. The smell was so strong, I had to leave.

Well, when the place couldn't hold any more people, the duke gave a fellow a quarter and told him to watch the door for a minute or two. Then he started for the stage door. I quickly followed him and when we turned the corner, he whispered, "Walk fast until

Huck Smells All Sorts of Foul Things.

you get away from town. Then run for the raft as fast as you can!"

I did just that, and so did he. We both got to the raft at the same moment. The king was already there. He had never even gone to town that night.

We didn't dare show a light until we were about ten miles below the village. Then we lit candles and had supper. The king and the duke fairly laughed their bones loose over the way they had tricked those people.

"Dummies!" cried the duke. "I knew the first house would keep mum and let the rest of the town get roped in. I also knew they'd try to get us on the third night, figuring it was their turn now. Well, it is their turn. Ha! I'd love to know what they're doing with all those rotten vegetables! Maybe they've decided to have a picnic!"

Those cheats took in four hundred sixty-five dollars in three nights. I never saw

Running for the Raft

money hauled in like that before.

By and by, when they were asleep and snoring inside the tent, Jim said, "Doesn't it surprise you the way this king and this duke carry on, Huck?"

"No," I answered.

"Why not, Huck?"

"Well, because it seems to be in the breed. I reckon they're all alike."

"But they're nothing but regular crooks," argued Jim.

"Well, that's what I'm saying. All kings and dukes are crooks, as far as I can make out."

All of Jim's dreams of royalty were shattered. He didn't say anything more. The sound of the river gently hitting the raft was all I heard.

Shattered Dreams of Royalty

Laying Up Under a Little Willow

CHAPTER 9

The Shameful Scheme

The next night, we laid up under a little willow growing out in the middle of the river. There were villages along both banks, and the duke and the king began to lay out plans for working all of them. They wanted to try the "Nonesuch" Tragedy again because there was so much money in it. But they figured it wouldn't be safe because the news might have spread by now. Since they couldn't agree on a project, the duke said he would rest for a day and work his brains for a while. The king decided to drop over to another village without any plan and just trust in Providence to lead him the profitable way.

We had all bought store clothes at our last stop. The king put on his and made quite a fuss over them. The king's duds were all black, and he looked mighty fine and starchy in them. But when he had on that white beaver coat, he looked so grand and good, no one would ever suspect that he was just a low down crook.

Jim cleaned up the canoe so the king wouldn't get dirty, and I got my paddle ready. Then we saw a big steamboat laying at the shore about three miles above the town. Since the king was so well dressed, he decided it would look better if we arrived at the town on the steamboat rather than in the canoe.

So he had me paddle him up river to meet the steamboat. I didn't have to be convinced

The King Looks Grand in His Beaver Coat.

to take a steamboat ride. That was a treat for anyone living along the Mississippi.

As we paddled up river close to shore, I spotted a young, innocent-looking country boy sitting on a log and swabbing the sweat off his face. A couple of big carpetbags sat on the river bank beside him.

The king had me steer the canoe towards the boy. "Where are you bound for?" the king called as we came close to the bank.

"I'm waiting for the steamboat to New Orleans," replied the boy.

The king gave him a big smile and invited him into our canoe. Since we were heading for the steamboat, we could take him there too.

The young chap thanked the king, then added, "When I first saw you, I said to myself, 'It's Mr. Wilks for sure. He came mighty close to getting here on time.' You aren't him, are you?"

134

A Country Boy on Shore

"No, I'm Reverend Alexander Blodgett," lied the king. "But tell me, lad, why did Mr. Wilks have to get here on time?" The king was becoming curious about this Mr. Wilks, and he began to pump the boy for all the information he could get.

The boy was only too happy to tell all he knew. It seemed that Mr. Wilks was due to arrive from England. His brother Peter had lived in this little town until his death two days ago. Peter hadn't seen his brothers, Harvey and William, since they were children in England. Peter had come to this country years ago with his brother George, who died some time ago, but his other two brothers still lived in England. Harvey was a preacher, and the poor unfortunate younger brother, William, was deaf and dumb.

The boy went on and on with the story. It seemed pretty boring to me, but the king was fascinated. You see, Peter Wilks had left

The King Pumps the Boy for Information.

behind a great deal of money. When he knew he was dying, he had written a letter to his brother Harvey in England, telling just where the money was hidden and giving him the rights to it. Peter's wife had died years ago, and he had no children. All he had in the whole world were his three nieces, George's daughters, and his two brothers over in England.

At this point I could see the king's mind working up sweat. He asked the boy all sorts of questions. How old were the three nieces? What did they look like? What were their names? He inquired about everybody and everything in that blessed town.

When he had finished questioning the boy, we dropped him off at the steamboat. The king never said anything about going aboard, so I lost my ride after all.

When the boat was gone, the king made me paddle up another mile to a deserted place

Dropping the Boy at the Steamboat

on the river bank. Then he and the duke went ashore. As he left, the king said to me, "Now hustle back and bring the new carpet-bags up here. And hurry!"

I knew what he was up to all right, but I never said a word. I did just what he told me. When I got back with the bags, the king and duke were sitting on a log talking about what the young boy had told them. All the while the king was talking, he tried to look and talk like an Englishman. He did it pretty well too. Then he asked the duke if he could pretend he was deaf and dumb. The duke said he was a master at that. So then they waited for the next steamboat.

About the middle of the afternoon, a big boat came up the river. They hailed it, and we went aboard. We only had to go about five miles. This made the captain pretty angry, what with having to stop and all, but the king gave him a few extra dollars to soothe

Making Plans to be Englishmen

his temper.

When the people in the village saw the big steamboat, they flocked to the shore. The first thing the king did when he got on the land was to walk up to a group of men and ask, "Excuse me, can any of you gentlemen tell me where Mr. Peter Wilks lives?"

The men glanced at one another and nodded their heads as if to say, "What did I tell you?" Then one of them said real gently, "Poor Mr. Wilks has just passed away."

Before I could turn around, the king went all to pieces. He fell against one of the men, put his head on the man's shoulder, and cried down his back.

Then he turned around, blubbering, and made a lot of idiotic signs with his hands to the duke. The duke immediately fell on one of the men and burst out crying too. If they weren't the meanest lot that I ever saw!

The King and the Duke Go to Pieces.

The Nieces Hug Their "Uncles."

CHAPTER 10

The Plan Begins to Work

Well, when we got up to the town, everybody was waiting for us. Pretty soon we were in the midle of a crowd. Every minute someone would yell, "Is it them?"

When we got to Peter Wilks' house, the three nieces were waiting for us. Mary Jane, the oldest, was so beautiful, it almost knocked my eyes out.

Anyway, the duke and the king continued their game, hugging the girls and making out like they were real miserable about the death and all.

The king blabbed along and managed to inquire about pretty much everybody and everything in town, including the dogs. He mentioned all sorts of little things that had happened at one time or another in the town. He pretended that his brother Peter had written him all these things in a letter. Of course, it was all a lie. All the information he had, he had gotten from that young boy in the boat.

Then Mary Jane fetched a letter her uncle had left behind. The king read it out loud and cried over it. It gave the house and three thousand dollars in gold to the girls and everything else to the two brothers. It also told where six thousand dollars in gold was hidden down in the basement.

So the two frauds said they'd go down and bring it up and have everything square and above board. They had pretended I was their servant, so they asked me to come along and

Mary Jane Fetches Her Uncle's Letter.

hold a candle for them. We shut the cellar door behind us and went downstairs. When they found the bag, they split it open on the floor. Gold coins fell like rain. My, the king's eyes did shine!

Most everyone would have been satisfied with the pile, but not these two. They had to count it. And count it, they did! But it came out four hundred dollars short of the six thousand. They looked all around for the four hundred dollars, but couldn't find it anywhere. Then they got to worrying. It wouldn't look good if the old man had said there was six thousand dollars, and now all they had come up with was five thousand six hundred.

So the duke got an idea. He took out the money they had made in the "Nonesuch" scheme and added it to the pile. Now, both men were just smiling away. They brought the money upstairs and insisted it be counted right then and there. They were

Gold Coins Fall Like Rain.

both pretending to be so honest and good, it nearly made me sick.

Then the king started going on in his English accent about how much he loved his dear departed brother and how much it meant for him to be here with the girls.

In the middle of this speech, one of the men laughed right in his face. Everyone was shocked. They tried to tell this man, whose name was Doctor Robinson, that these men were Peter Wilks' brothers and they had just come in from England.

But the Doctor looked everyone in the face and said, "Englishmen, ha! Why anyone could tell that these two fakes are no more English than you or I." Then he looked at the girls and added, "I was your uncle's friend and an honest one too. I only want to protect you and keep you from harm and trouble. These men are imposters. Don't let them take you for fools."

"Englishmen, Ha!"

Well, the people tried to quiet the doctor down, but he just wouldn't listen to them. They explained how the king had known every little thing about the town and the family, and how he was such an honest man and all that.

Mary Jane straightened herself up and said, "Here is my answer!" With that, she shoved the bag of money into the king's hands, saying, "Take our three thousand dollars from the six and invest it for me and my sisters any way you want to, and don't give us any receipt!"

The king had a big smile on his face.

But the doctor angrily shouted, "All right! I wash my hands of the matter. But I warn you that the time will come when you'll feel sick thinking of this day."

"All right, doctor," said the king. "If they ever feel sick, we'll try and get them to send for you then!"

Mary Jane Gives the King the Money.

A Room for the King

CHAPTER 11

Exposing the Frauds

When everyone had left the house, the king asked Mary Jane if she had a spare room or two. She had only one, which she gave the king. But she gave up her own room for the duke and put me in a little attic room.

So Mary Jane took us up and showed us the rooms, which were plain but nice. She said she'd take out her dresses and things so that everyone would have enough space and be real comfortable.

When I was finally alone, I got a chance to think about things. Mary Jane and her sisters were real decent folks. I just couldn't live with myself if I let those crooks trick them out of everything they had.

On the other hand, if the duke or the king every caught me telling the truth, who knows what they might do! It was a difficult situation all around. My old friend Tom Sawyer would have known what to do. He had a great mind for thinking up plans and schemes. This was one time when I really could have used old Tom!

So I started to think real hard. There was only one way out. If I could steal the money, I would hide it. Then, after I was gone, I would write Mary Jane a letter and tell her where it was hidden. It was the only way, and I had to do it soon.

So I crept downstairs in the dark and began to search the rooms. I went right to the king's room because I knew he wouldn't trust anyone but himself with the gold. It was

Huck Searches the King's Room.

pitch dark, but I poked around quite a bit. Pretty soon I found the bag under some things in the closet. Just as I was about to leave, I heard the king and the duke coming up the stairs. I hid under the bed, but I could hear them whispering.

"Let's leave right away," said the duke.

"That's foolish," answered the king. "We have plenty of time."

Anyway, the king convinced the duke, and the two turned to go into another room. I grabed my chance and ran downstairs as quickly as I could. I just wanted to hide the money somewhere temporarily, so that I could move it later. I looked around everywhere. Then I walked into the room where the body of Peter Wilks was laying in the coffin. It gave me the chills.

Just then, I heard someone coming down the stairs. In a moment of panic, I shoved the bag of gold coins under the lid of the coffin,

Hiding the Gold in the Coffin

then ran back across the room and hid behind the door.

Mary Jane entered the room. She sat by her poor dead uncle's coffin and cried her heart out. It hurt me to see her without her uncle and without her money too. As soon as she left, I made a decision—I had to tell her everything.

I took a candle and walked up to her room. I knocked once, and she let me in. Her eyes were all red, but she still looked beautiful. The story just poured out of me. It seemed I just couldn't stop myself. I told her how the king and the duke were just two lowdown crooks and how they had learned everything about her and her sisters and the town from that young lad we had picked up in the canoe.

She looked real upset and was about to begin crying again. But I told her that her money was safe and that she could rest easy.

Mary Jane Hears Huck's Confession.

Of course, I couldn't bear to tell her that I had hidden it in her uncle's coffin, so I decided to wait with that part of my story.

Next, I made her promise not to breathe a word of what I had told her until it was safe. We had to expose the frauds first, and I had just the plan to do it. She agreed to remain mum for a little while. I knew I'd need some time to get away myself and to get back to the raft and to Jim. But of course, I couldn't tell her all this. So all I said was, "It's a rough gang, those two frauds, and I'm involved pretty deep, so I've got to travel with them a while longer, whether I want to or not. I'd rather not tell you why. You see there is another person that you don't know who would be in big trouble if we exposed everything right now."

Mary Jane had tears in her eyes. She took my hand and thanked me again and again. Well, I got so nervous, I started stammering.

Mary Jane Thanks Huck.

Then I said good night and walked slowly back to my room.

The first thing in the morning, the front door bell rang. Next thing I knew, Dr. Robinson was standing there with two nice-looking old gentlemen. The older one started to speak, and right away I could tell that he pronounced things like a real Englishman.

Dr. Robinson introduced the two men. "Here are the real brothers of Peter Wilks. They just arrived today. Their journey was interrupted by a storm at sea. These men are not imposters, and they have proof of their identity!"

I couldn't believe my eyes! This saved me a lot of trouble, for I hadn't thought of a real good way yet to prove that the king and the duke were fakes.

But the two crooks just froze there and looked the Englishmen right square in the eyes. Then the king stood up real straight

The Real Brothers of Peter Wilks.

and said, "Storm at sea, my foot! You can't discredit us. We are the true heirs to the fortune!"

I couldn't believe the nerve of those two. In a few minutes, a whole crowd had gathered around the house. Mary Jane kept her promise to me and didn't say a thing, although I could see she was busting to tell all that she knew.

Next thing, the town lawyer showed up. He demanded proof of identity from the two Englishmen. But it seemed that in the storm, some of the Englishmen's baggage had been lost, and they were still waiting for a steamboat to come with their proper documents.

This gave the king more fuel for his fire, and he went on and on about how these men were the imposters and that no one could possibly believe such a wild story as theirs.

Then the white-haired gentleman from England asked the king a simple question.

The King Calls the Men Imposters.

"Tell me now, if you are really Peter Wilks' brother, what sort of tattoo did Peter have on his chest?"

The king thought a minute, then said, "It was a tiny blue arrow."

The gentleman turned to the undertaker and said, "There, you've heard what he said! Was there any such mark on Peter Wilks' chest?"

The undertaker shook his head and said, "Why no, I never saw a blue arrow."

"Good!" said the gentleman. "Now I'll tell you. My brother had the initials P-B-W tattooed on his chest. They were tattooed there when he was just a lad."

But the undertaker said he didn't recall seeing any marks at all on Peter Wilks' chest.

Well, everyone was in a state now. They were whopping and hollering at once.

"They're both frauds!"

"Let's drown 'em all!"

"They're Both Frauds!"

"Let's ride 'em out of town on a rail!"

But the lawyer jumped up on the table and yelled, "Gentlemen, hear me out. Just a single word, if you please. There's one sure way to tell who is telling the truth. Let's go inside and open the coffin and take a look."

Then I knew it was all over for the king and the duke. I knew the lawyer and Mary Jane would find the money, and she would tell all that I had told her.

As the angry crowd surged into the house, I saw my chance and lit out the back door. I had the road to myself, and I fairly flew towards the shore. I grabbed the first boat I could find and set out for the raft.

It was beginning to storm now, and a flash of lightning revealed the raft. I was so happy at the sight of it that I could barely hold back the tears.

"Jim! Jim!" I cried. "We're free of them! Come on out!"

Huck Lights Out the Back Door.

Huck Can't Find Jim.

CHAPTER 12

Tom Sawyer Arrives

Jim wasn't on the raft. I knew in a minute what had happened. Someone must have spotted the raft and figured Jim was a runaway slave. Whoever it was had probably taken Jim into town to collect the reward money. I felt terrible. Jim was my friend. And even though I knew slavery was legal and all, in my heart I had always hoped Jim would escape to a free state.

Now, because he had waited for me, because he was a loyal friend, he had been caught. My mind was all a jumble. I knew it wasn't right to break the law, but I just had to save poor Jim. I got to thinking about our trip down the river and how Jim and I had been together for so long. I could see him sitting by me, singing and laughing and doing nice things for me. Yes sir, even if it would be against the law, I was going to find Jim and help him escape to freedom!

The first thing that had to be done was to find out where they were keeping Jim. That wouldn't be so hard to do. In this part of the country, a runaway slave was always big news. Someone would be sure to know where he was.

But I couldn't do anything that night, so I tied up the raft and slept until morning. First thing I did when the sun came up was to walk into town. It was a dusty, hot little place. Children were playing in the dirt road, and a couple of farmers were loading feed into wagons. I didn't want to appear too

A Dusty, Hot Town

obvious, so I walked around for a spell.

Finally, I sat down by one of the farmers and started shooting the breeze.

The farmer began talking about the crops and all. Pretty soon he mentioned that some fellow had caught a runaway slave drifting down the river on a wooden raft. I acted like I didn't hear him. So he repeated the story a second time, only this time he said the man's name. It was Phelps—Silas Phelps, a farmer from the next county. Phelps was holding Jim until he could find out more about him.

As soon as I could get away without arousing the farmer's suspicion, I did. I started through the woods towards the next county.

When I got there, it was all still and Sunday-like, hot and sunshiny. Everyone was in the fields, and there was a faint buzzing of bugs and flies in the air. It was lonesome, and it seemed like everybody was dead.

Phelps' plantation was one of those little

Shooting the Breeze with a Farmer

one-horse cotton farms. It looked just like all the other cotton farms along the road. I went towards the house, not fixing up any particular plan, but just trusting in fate to put the right words in my mouth when the time came. Just then, a woman came running out the front door. She was all smiling and happy-looking and waving her hand.

"It's you, at last! Isn't it?" she called.

Before I had time to think, I answered, "Yes, ma'am, it is!"

The woman grabbed me and hugged me tight. She shook and shook, and the tears ran down her cheeks.

"Dear, dear cousin Tom. I've waited so long to see you. Wherever have you been?"

She didn't even give me a chance to answer, which was good, before she started asking me all sorts of questions... Where was my baggage? How was the trip? What had taken so long? Was everyone back home all right?

"It's You, At Last!"

My mind could hardly-keep up with her, but then I realized I had to come up with some answers.

"My bags are at the depot, ma'am," I explained, "and the steamboat had engine trouble. That's why I'm late."

When she invited me into the house, I began to get real uneasy. The questions were getting harder and harder to answer. There were children all around, and she introduced me to each one as "Cousin Tom." I wanted to get the kids to one side to pump them a little and find out who I was, but it was impossible. The woman just talked a blue streak. At one point, she referred to herself as "Aunt Sally," so at least I knew what to call her.

Finally Aunt Sally stopped for a breath, but then she went on. "Well, here I am a-running on this way, and you haven't told me a word about Sis or any of them. Now I'll rest a

Aunt Sally Talks a Blue Streak.

little, and you start up on your news. Just tell me everything about everyone."

Well, I could see I was in trouble now. I was just about to throw up my hands and admit everything when she grabbed me and pushed me behind a bed.

"Here he comes!" she cried. "Hide under here and we'll surprise him!"

I was really in a fix now. Her husband was coming home, and she wanted to surprise him. I had just one little glimpse of old Mr. Phelps when he came in, then the bed hid him.

Mrs. Phelps ran to greet her husband, asking, "Has he come?"

"No," said her husband.

"Goodness gracious!" she cried. "What in the world could have become of him?"

Then she led the old man to the window. While his back was turned, she stooped down at the foot of the bed and gave me a pull. Out

"Hide and We'll Surprise Him!"

I came. When Mr. Phelps turned back from the window, there she stood, beaming and smiling like a house on fire.

The old gentleman looked at me and asked, "Why, who's that?"

Mrs. Phelps smiled and said, "Why it's Tom Sawyer, that's who!"

I almost slumped through the floor! So that's who I was supposed to be—only my best friend in the whole world! The old man shook my hand again and again, and the woman laughed and cried at the same time.

I was just as happy to find out who I was as they were happy to see me. For the next two hours I answered all the questions they had about Aunt Polly, Sis, and Tom's half-brother Sid. Now, I was feeling pretty good. Being Tom Sawyer was easy and comfortable, and it stayed easy and comfortable until I heard a steamboat coughing along down the river. Then I said to myself, "Suppose Tom Sawyer

184

"It's Tom Sawyer, That's Who!"

comes down on that boat? And suppose he steps in here any minute and sings out my name before I can throw him a wink to keep quiet?"

Well, I couldn't let that happen, so I told the folks that I was going into town to fetch my baggage. Mr. Phelps wanted to go along with me, but I managed to talk him out of it.

I started for town in Mr. Phelps' wagon, and when I was halfway there, I saw a wagon coming towards me. Sure enough, it was Tom Sawyer! I stopped and waited till he came alongside.

"Hold on!" I shouted.

Tom's mouth opened up like he'd seen a ghost. He swallowed two or three times like a person who's got a dry throat, then he said, "I haven't done you any harm. You know that. So, then what do you want to come back and haunt me for?"

Tom really thought I was a ghost. He really

Tom Thinks Huck Is a Ghost.

believed I had died in the river. I had to laugh. Then I explained that I really was alive and told him everything that had happened on the river. Then I told him why I was here.

"I want to steal Jim away and set him free," I said.

I wasn't sure how Tom would react. He liked adventure all right, but Tom usually didn't do anything illegal. But his eyes lit up and he said, "Huck, I'll help you steal him!"

I was shocked. I never thought Tom would offer to help. This really was great news. So then I took Tom's trunk and put it in my wagon. We agreed that Tom would come up to the house later and pretend he was his own half-brother, Sid. That way, we could both stay at the Phelps' house and work out a plan to set Jim free.

When I got back to the house, dinner was all ready, and the whole family was waiting

Tom Agrees to Help Huck Steal Jim.

for me. About half an hour later, Tom's wagon drove up, and Aunt Sally saw it through the window. She thought it was some stranger. Being the kind, generous people they were, Aunt Sally and her husband invited Tom inside.

Tom waited till they had set a place for him at the table, then he confessed that he was Sid and that he had wanted to come. So his mother had finally given in, and he had taken the next boat out of town.

Well, there really was a celebration then! Aunt Sally didn't know what to do first. The kids all danced around, and it was like one big family party!

We had dinner out in the backyard. There was enough food on that table for seven families. Everything was hot and freshly made too. But the whole time I kept thinking about where Jim might be and about looking for him as soon as possible.

190

A Family Dinner

Huck Describes His Adventures.

CHAPTER 13

Tom Plans Jim's Escape

That night, Tom told me how everyone reckoned I was murdered and how Pap disappeared pretty soon after and how no one had ever seen him since. I filled Tom in on all the details of the "Nonesuch" scheme and our adventures on the raft. Then we got to talking about where Jim could be hidden.

"Looky here, Huck, what fools we are not to think of it before!" cried Tom. "I bet I know where Jim is!"

"But how could you?" I asked.

"Well, Hucky, on my way here, I saw a

slave go into a hut down by the edge of the plantation. He was carrying food. The hut had a lock on it, and a lock meant there had to be a prisoner. So the food had to be for the prisoner."

What a head for just a boy to have! If I had Tom Sawyer's head, I wouldn't trade it to be a duke or a mate on a steamboat or a clown in a circus. I knew pretty well that Tom would think of some complicated plan to free Jim.

And sure enough, after a while Tom said he wanted to think of a wonderful, mysterious way to get Jim out of the hut.

"Why not just saw a hole in the wall and let Jim slip on out?" I suggested.

But Tom only laughed. "There has to be a more interesting way than that to get him out," he said. He thought for a while, then cried out, "I have it! We'll dig a tunnel to get him out. It will be a hard job, but at least it

Tom Saw a Slave Carry Food into a Hut.

will be more mysterious and more complicated than just sawing a hole."

So we talked some more about Tom's plan, and then we decided that we had to go and see Jim.

We waited for the slave who carried the food to the hut, then followed him. Tom gave him a dime, and he let us in to see Jim. Of course we didn't tell him we knew Jim. We simply acted as though we were curious to see what a real runaway slave looked like.

Jim was real happy to see us. He practically cried for joy. But before Jim could say a word, Tom leaned over and whispered, "Don't ever let on that you know us. And if you hear any digging going on during the night, it's us. We're going to set you free."

Jim grabbed both of us by the hands and squeezed real hard, so we knew how thankful he was.

The next morning, Tom was upset about

A Dime to See a Real Runaway Slave

the plan.

"Blame it!" he cried. "This whole thing is just as easy as it can be. There's nothing wonderful or mysterious about it. It sure is difficult to think up a complicated plan. There isn't any watchman to be drugged. There isn't even a dog to give a sleeping mixture to. And there's Jim chained by one leg with a ten-foot chain to the leg of his bed. Why, all we have to do is lift up the bedstead and slip off the chain. Why, drat it, Huck, it's the stupidest arrangement I've ever seen. We have to invent all the difficulties and dangers ourselves. Well, we'll just have to do the best we can with the materials we've got, but we've got to get a saw."

When I asked why he needed a saw, Tom got real angry.

"What do we want with a saw? Don't we have to saw off the leg of Jim's bed so we can get the chain loose?"

Tom Wants a More Complicated Plan.

The Adventures of Huckleberry Finn

It was clear to me now that Tom wouldn't do anything the easy way if there was a more complicated method available. In addition to the saw he also needed sheets to make a rope ladder. The fact that Jim could easily have reached the ground from the hut didn't matter to Tom one bit.

That night we began digging under the hut. The work was hard and sweaty, but after about two and a half hours the job was done. We crept in under Jim's bed and into the cabin. Tom brought a candle which we lit, and then we stood looking at Jim as he slept. He looked hearty and healthy. We woke him up gently. He was so glad to see us he almost cried. He thought we were going to sneak him out that night, but Tom showed him how uninteresting that would be. Then he sat down and told him all about our plans and how we could change them in a minute any time there was an alarm. He assured

Digging Under the Hut

Jim that everything would go smoothly and not to be afraid of anything.

So Jim said it was all right, and we sat there for a while and talked over old times. Jim told us that Mr. and Mrs. Phelps came in to see him every day and that they were very kind and gave him plenty to eat.

That night Tom added some extra frills to his plans. He wrote a letter and shoved it under Aunt Sally's front door. The letter said:

BEWARE. TROUBLE IS BREWING. KEEP A SHARP LOOKOUT.

UNKNOWN FRIEND

Tom said this would make the whole escape much more exciting and dangerous.

The next night, Tom drew a picture of a skull and crossbones in blood, and we stuck it on the front door. And the next night, he drew another one of a coffin and stuck it on the back door. Everyone was in a sweat.

If a door banged, Aunt Sally jumped and

Tom Tells Jim Not to Be Afraid.

cried, "Ouch!" If anything fell, she screamed. So the thing was working very well. Tom said he never saw a thing work more satisfactory.

Now he said it was time for the big move! So the very next morning at daybreak, we got another letter ready. But now, Mr. Phelps had guards at all the doors. Aunt Sally had gotten so frightened that she made her husband have a slave stand watch at each door, day and night.

But Tom waited until he saw one of the slaves fall asleep. Then he slipped the letter under the front mat. This letter was longer. It said:

DON'T BETRAY ME. I WISH TO BE YOUR FRIEND. THERE IS A DESPERATE GANG OF CUTTHROATS FROM OVER IN THE INDIAN TERRITORY WHO ARE PLANNING TO STEAL THE RUNAWAY SLAVE TONIGHT. THEY HAVE BEEN TRYING TO SCARE YOU, SO THAT YOU WILL STAY IN THE HOUSE

Tom Slips a Letter Under the Mat.

AND NOT BOTHER THEM. I AM ONE OF THE GANG.
BUT NOW I HAVE GOTTEN RELIGION AND WANT
TO DO THE RIGHT THING. THEY WILL SNEAK
DOWN FROM THE NORTH ALONG THE FENCE AT
MIDNIGHT. THEY HAVE A FALSE KEY AND WILL
GO INTO THE HUT AND STEAL THE SLAVE. SLIP
INTO THE HUT AND LOCK THEM IN. DON'T DO
ANYTHING BUT WHAT I HAVE TOLD YOU HERE. I
ONLY WANT TO DO THE RIGHT THING.

UNKNOWN FRIEND

Once the letter was hidden under the front
mat, Tom quietly tiptoed back into the house
and up to bed.

Tiptoeing up to Bed

Fishing on the River

CHAPTER 14

The Getaway

We were feeling pretty good after breakfast, so we took my canoe and went out on the river. We fished a little and had lunch. When we got home, everyone was so worried, they didn't know which end was up. They made us go right to our rooms after supper and never let on a word about the letter.

About eleven o'clock, Tom slipped out the window and headed for the hut. I went down to the cellar to get some last-minute provisions. When I came back up the stairs and walked into the sitting room, I nearly fainted! My, but there was a crowd in there! Fifteen farmers, and every one of them had a gun. I was so powerful sick that I slunk to a chair. Everyone was real nervous. Obviously they had all gathered to try and catch the gang that was planning to free Jim. It was about this time that I realized that Tom's sense of adventure had gone too far.

Anyway, when Aunt Sally saw me, she scolded me for leaving my room and sent me straight back upstairs.

I was upstairs in a second and out the window in another one. I ran to the hut faster than I ever thought it was possible. I could hardly get my words out I was so anxious. I told Tom as quickly as I could that we didn't have a minute to lose. His eyes just blazed with excitement, and I could see that he wasn't scared at all.

In a few seconds, we could hear the tramp of men coming to the door, and then we

Huck Sneaks Out the Window.

heard them fumble with the padlock. Next thing we knew, they were inside. Tom, Jim, and I crept under the bed and slid out through the hole we had dug.

We crept through the darkness to the fence which surrounded the plantation. Jim and I got over it in no time, but Tom's britches caught on a splinter on the top rail. As he tried to pull loose, the splinter snapped and made a noise. Next thing we heard was someone shouting, "Who's that? Answer or I'll shoot!"

But we didn't answer. We just jumped up and ran. Then there was a rush and a bang! bang! bang! And the bullets fairly whizzed around us! We heard the men shout, "There they are! Set the dogs loose!"

We followed the path to the river. Soon the dogs caught up with us, but they were *our* dogs, so we stopped in our tracks till they caught up with us. When they saw it was

Tom's Britches Catch on the Rail.

only us, they sniffed a bit, then continued running along the path away from us, barking and clattering.

We followed the path to the canoe and hopped in. We pulled for dear life towards the middle of the river. Then we struck out easy and comfortable for the island where my raft was.

In the background we could hear the men yelling and the dogs barking at each other all up and down the bank. Soon we were so far away that the sounds got dim and died out. As soon as I could step up on the raft, I sat down next to Jim real proud and spoke.

"Now, Jim, you're a free man, and I bet you won't ever be a slave again."

We were all as glad as could be, but Tom was the gladdest. Then Tom told us some awful news. He had a bullet in his calf! Suddenly Jim and me, we didn't feel as brave as we had before. The wound was hurting Tom

"Now, Jim, You're a Free Man."

considerably, and it was bleeding too. We laid him down and tore up a shirt to bandage the wound. But Tom wanted to do everything himself. He thought it was all part of the adventure. I wasn't so sure.

"What do you think we should do, Jim?" I asked.

"Well, Huck, I don't think we should budge a step until we get a proper doctor to fix Tom's leg."

I knew it might ruin everything, but we had think of Tom now. So I told Jim to run and lie in the woods. Then I made Tom comfortable on the raft and tied the raft up to a tree on the bank. I took the canoe and crossed the river to town to find a doctor.

It wasn't hard finding the doctor's house. In small towns everyone knows just where the doctor lives. I knocked on the door and told him that my brother and I were over on Spanish Island hunting and that my brother

Bandaging Tom's Bullet Wound

must have kicked his gun while he was napping, because it went off and shot him in the leg. I asked the doctor to fix it so that we could go home without worrying our folks.

The doctor looked kind of curious, but he got his bag and followed me to the canoe. He took one look at the canoe and said, "I'm not sure it's safe for the two of us."

"But doctor," I said, "we rowed to the island in it."

"Well, son, I don't trust it. Suppose you wait here on shore while I go tend to your brother."

I couldn't argue with him, but as he rowed off, I got to thinking. Suppose it took a couple of days for the doctor to fix up Tom's leg? What was I going to do? Lay around here until he got better? No sir!

That's when I decided that if the doctor had to take care of Tom for a few days, then I would be there too. What if that doctor let

Getting Help from a Doctor

the cat out of the bag about Jim? Then Jim would be in real trouble, and he would never be a free man again. I just had to get back to the island and see what was up.

But it was too late that night to get back to the island, so I just crept into a lumber pile near the river to get a little sleep. When I woke up, the sun was away up over my head. I shot out and went for the doctor's house, but they told me he'd gone away in the night some time or other and he wasn't back yet. Well, I began to think that this looked real bad for Tom. I'd better head for the island right away. So I began heading out of town towards the river. Just as I turned a corner, I nearly walked right into Mr. Phelps!

"Why, Tom! Where have you been all this time, you rascal? Everyone has been real worried about where you and Sid had gone."

My mind worked like lightning. I said, "Oh, we're fine. We followed the men and the

Huck Meets Mr. Phelps.

dogs, but they outran us, and we lost them. Then we thought we heard them on the water, so we got a canoe and took out after them. We crossed over, but couldn't find anything. Then we cruised upshore till we got kind of tired, and we tied up the canoe and went to sleep. We just woke up an hour ago and paddled over here to hear the news. Sid's at the post office to see what he can hear."

When we went to the post office to get "Sid," of course he wasn't there. We waited a while, but soon Mr. Phelps got tired of waiting around. He made me go back home with him, even though I told him I wanted to wait around for "Sid."

When we got home, Aunt Sally was so glad to see me that she laughed and cried at the same time. The house was full of people, talking and speculating about the gang and the runaway slave and all the exciting news.

Well, after we had finished dinner, there

Waiting for "Sid."

was still no sign of "Sid." Aunt Sally was beside herself with worry. She sent some men into the town to scout around for him.

And then when I went up to bed, she fetched her candle and came up with me. She tucked me in and mothered me so good, I felt mean. I couldn't look her in the face. She sat down on the bed and talked with me for a long time. She talked about what a fine boy "Sid" was, and if I reckoned he could have gotten lost or hurt or even drowned. The tears dripped slowly from her eyes, and I felt so bad, I almost told her everything. And then when she was leaving, she looked down in my eyes so steady and gentle and said, "The door isn't going to be locked, Tom, and there's the window, but you'll be good, won't you. . .for my sake?"

I wanted to go so badly, but after what she said, I just couldn't leave the house. Still, Tom was on my mind so, I hardly slept at all.

"You'll Be Good, Won't You?"

The Procession

CHAPTER 15

Tom's Confession

Mr. Phelps went back to town again before breakfast, but he couldn't find any trace of Tom. He and Aunt Sally just sat at the table, thinking and not saying a word. Their coffee was cold in the cups, and the food was untouched. Suddenly, Aunt Sally saw something. She jumped up and ran towards the window. So did I.

There was a procession coming towards the house. It was the doctor, then Jim with his hands tied behind his back, then a crowd of people carrying Tom Sawyer on a mattress.

Aunt Sally flung herself at Tom, crying, "Oh, he's dead, I just know it!"

But Tom turned his head a little and muttered something or other, which showed he was still breathing. Then they took him into the house to put him to bed.

I followed the men to see what they were going to do with Jim. Some of them wanted to hang Jim as an example to all the other slaves, but others were against it, even though they were cussing Jim considerably.

But the whole time, Jim never let on that he knew me or anything about what Tom and I had done. Meanwhile, the men put Jim back in the hut, and this time they chained his arms and legs to the bed and had a couple of farmers stand watch in front of the place.

By and by, the doctor came out of the house and said that Tom was going to be all right, but that it was Jim who had really saved Tom's life.

Jim Is Chained to the Bed.

"When I got to the island," he said, "I saw I couldn't remove the bullet without some help. But the boy wasn't in any condition for me to leave and get help. He was getting worse and worse. I knew I couldn't do anything at all by myself, so I said out loud, 'If only I had help!'

"Somehow, the minute I said it, out crawls this slave from nowhere and says he'll help. And he did too. He did it very well, I might add. Anyway, I knew he must be a runaway, so I took him back with me. But never once did he try to get away or leave this boy's side. He's a faithful man, that he is!"

Well, then everyone softened up a little, and I was mighty thankful to that old doctor for doing Jim that good turn.

Then I got to wondering about how I was going to explain Tom's being shot and me not saying anything to anybody. But I had plenty of time, because Aunt Sally stuck to the sick-room all day and all night. And every time I

"If Only I Had Help!"

saw her husband, I avoided him.

Next morning, when I heard that Tom was a good deal better and Aunt Sally had gone to take a nap, I slipped in to see him. But he was sleeping, and sleeping very peacefully too. He was pale, not fire-faced the way he was when they had brought him in. So I sat down and waited for him to wake up. But just as he began to stir, in walked Aunt Sally.

When Tom opened his eyes, he began to talk. And talk he did! Why he bragged and bragged and told Aunt Sally what a splendid job we did in freeing Jim and how we planned and prepared and how exciting it all was!

Aunt Sally couldn't believe her ears! "Well, I never heard the likes of it in all my born days!" she cried. "So it *was* you, you rapscallions, that's been making all this trouble and turning everybody's wits clean inside out and

Tom Brags About Freeing Jim.

scaring us all to death!"

But Tom was only concerned about one thing—Jim. And Aunt Sally explained that Jim was safe and sound and bound hand and foot in the hut.

"They haven't any right to shut him up!" shouted Tom. "Turn him loose! He isn't a slave; he's as free as any creature on this earth! Old Miss Watson, his mistress, died two months ago, and she was so ashamed of her plans to sell him down the river that she set him free in her will!"

"Then what on earth did you want to set him free for, seeing that he was already free?" asked Aunt Sally.

"Why, for the adventure of it!" answered Tom.

Just then, Aunt Polly, Tom's aunt from back home, appeared at the door. Now the whole game was up for sure. She had taken the steamboat all the way from St.

Aunt Polly Appears.

Petersburg to find out what had been going on. First thing she did was look at me and say, "Huck Finn, what on earth are you doing here?"

Poor Aunt Sally didn't know what to think. All this time she thought that I was Tom and that Tom was Sid. Well, finally Tom and I confessed everything. There was no use trying to cover it up. Aunt Polly confirmed Tom's story about Jim.

So as soon as they could, the men set Jim free, and he came to the sickroom to visit Tom. Aunt Sally gave him a good meal, and we all sat around and talked. Tom gave Jim forty dollars for being prisoner for us and for doing it so well.

And then Tom and Jim and I talked on and on. After a while, I saw that old look come into Tom's eye. He had a plan again.

"Why don't all three of us sneak out one night and get outfits and go for a howling

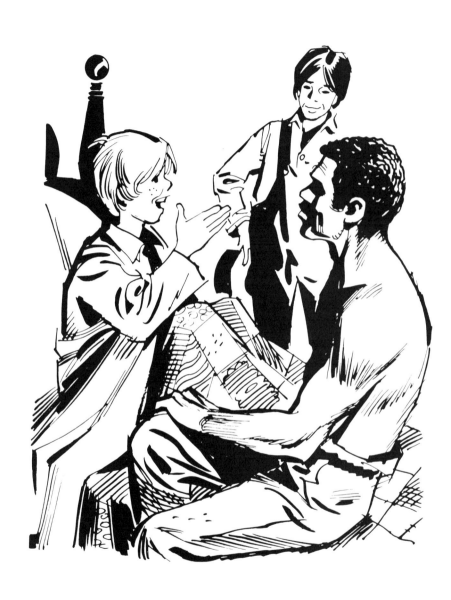

Tom Has New Plans.

adventure among the Indians over in the territory?"

"That sounds just fine, Tom," I said, "but I don't have any money to buy an outfit. I reckon that Pap has been to Judge Thatcher and gotten all of my money by now."

It was then that Jim told me that while we were on Jackson's Island, he had seen a house float by. Inside the house he had seen Pap's body. So Pap was dead, and the money was mine.

Tom's well now, and he's got his bullet on a chain around his neck. The adventure is all over, and there's nothing more to write about. I'm glad of it, because if I'd have known what trouble it was to write a book, I wouldn't have tackled it. Now I'm going to head out to Indian territory ahead of the rest. Aunt Sally wants to adopt me and make me live in a house and be civilized. I tried it before and I can't stand it!

Tom Shows Off His Bullet.

B4825